Alexander McCall Smith is the author of over eighty books on a wide range of subjects. For many years he was Professor of Medical Law at the University of Edinburgh and worked with national and international organisations concerned with medical ethics. Then in 1999 he achieved world-wide recognition for his award-winning series of novels, The No.1 Ladies' Detective Agency. Since then, he has devoted his time to the writing of fiction, including the 44 Scotland Street and Corduroy Mansions series. His books have been translated into forty-six languages. He lives in Edinburgh with his wife, Elizabeth, a doctor.

Also by Alexander McCall Smith

The No.1 Ladies' Detective Agency Series
The No.1 Ladies' Detective Agency
Tears of the Giraffe
Morality for Beautiful Girls
The Kalahari Typing School for Men
The Full Cupboard of Life
In the Company of Cheerful Ladies
Blue Shoes and Happiness
The Good Husband of Zebra Drive
The Miracle at Speedy Motors
Tea Time for the Traditionally Built
The Double Comfort Safari Club
The Saturday Big Tent Wedding Party
The Limpopo Academy of Private Detection

The Sunday Philosophy Club Series
The Sunday Philosophy Club
Friends, Lovers, Chocolate
The Right Attitude to Rain
The Careful Use of Compliments
The Comfort of Saturdays
The Lost Art of Gratitude
The Charming Quirks of Others
The Forgotten Affairs of Youth

The 44 Scotland Street Series
44 Scotland Street
Espresso Tales
Love Over Scotland
The World According to Bertie
The Unbearable Lightness of Scones
The Importance of Being Seven

The Corduroy Mansions Series
Corduroy Mansions
The Dog Who Came in from the Cold

The von Igelfeld Entertainments
The 2½ Pillars of Wisdom
Unusual Uses for Olive Oil

La's Orchestra Saves the World

The Cleverness of Ladies

Alexander McCall Smith

O42990

ABACUS

First published in Great Britain in 2012 by Abacus
Reprinted 2012

A CIP catalogue record for this book
is available from the British Library.

ISBN 978-0-349-00028-2

Typeset in Stone Serif by M Rules
Printed and bound in Great Britain by
Clays Ltd, St Ives plc

Papers used by Abacus are from well-managed forests
and other responsible sources.

MIX
Paper from
responsible sources
FSC® C104740

Abacus
An imprint of
Little, Brown Book Group
100 Victoria Embankment
London EC4Y 0DY

An Hachette UK Company
www.hachette.co.uk

www.littlebrown.co.uk

The Cleverness of Ladies

1

It was a slack time at the No. 1 Ladies'
Detective Agency, the only detective agency in
Botswana. It would be wrong to say that
nothing was going on – Mma Ramotswe, who
had founded the agency to deal with the
problems of ladies (and others), knew that
something was always happening. People were
always getting themselves into unfortunate
scrapes; they had always done this, and human
nature showed no sign of changing. No, the
reason why things were quiet was that nobody
was bringing anything to the attention of the
small detective agency at the back of Tlokweng
Road Speedy Motors.

The garage business was owned by Mma
Ramotswe's husband, Mr J. L. B. Matekoni,
who everyone agreed was the finest mechanic
in Botswana. She had been engaged to Mr
J. L. B. Matekoni for rather a long time, and
eventually he had married her. But some say

this was only as a result of clever plotting by the cunning matron of the Tlokweng Orphan Farm, Mma Potokwani.

Yet such a view was uncharitable. Mr J. L. B. Matekoni was sometimes a bit indecisive, and marriage proved to be only one of the things that he was indecisive about. The important thing was that he did marry Mma Ramotswe eventually, and he had now moved into her house on Zebra Drive, a fine house with a shady veranda and a good vegetable garden to the rear.

They were very fortunate, and not a day went by without Mma Ramotswe reminding herself of this good fortune. When things were slack in the office, as they now were, she reminded herself of her good fortune rather more frequently. It was a very good way of preventing feelings of frustration, especially when there was nothing to do but look at the small white gecko which ran up the office wall and then, defying gravity, across the ceiling boards. But the trouble with thinking about one's good fortune was that, after a while, one began to wish to do something else, and that, of course, depended on the arrival of a client.

'Mma Ramotswe?' The voice which interrupted her was that of her assistant, Mma Makutsi. She had been busying herself filing papers, and was now looking intently at her employer. 'You look as if you're daydreaming.'

Mma Ramotswe nodded. 'I was, I suppose.'

'There is nothing wrong with that,' said Mma Makutsi. 'When you have nothing better to do.'

'Well,' said Mma Ramotswe. 'I don't.'

'Except now you do,' said Mma Makutsi. 'There is somebody coming, Mma. I can see him out there. He is coming to the door.'

Mma Ramotswe picked up a piece of paper and began to look at it closely. It did no harm for clients to think that one was busy, even when one was not. If the client thought that one had nothing to do, his confidence in the agency might be dented and that, in the long run, would not help. In the giving of advice to other people – which was what being a private detective was usually all about – it was important that the client believe in the detective. So there was nothing wrong, she felt, in picking up a piece of paper and pretending to be very busy reading it. Even if the paper was no more than a letter from one of Mr J. L. B. Matekoni's suppliers, saying that a set of spark plugs which he had ordered for the garage had now been received and was awaiting collection.

3

Mma Makutsi ushered in the client and pointed to the visitors' chair. 'That is where you must sit, Rra,' she said to the smartly dressed, middle-aged man. He had given her his name, but she had not caught it and did not wish to ask him again. There was something about this man which suggested authority. When he had introduced himself, he had had a look about him which implied that she should know exactly who he was in any case. There was something familiar about him, Mma Makutsi thought. Was he a politician? They often had that air of assurance that comes with the exercise of power, and they usually expected people to know who they were.

Mma Ramotswe looked at her visitor. She, too, was having difficulty placing him. With her detective's eye, always ready to pick up visual clues, she took in the expensive shoes and the gold buckle on his belt. These were not items that one could buy locally; they came from over the border – from Johannesburg, at the least, possibly from somewhere even more exotic such as London or New York. Was he a businessman? There was a number of prosperous businessmen in Gaborone these days, but most of them were reasonably well known because they had their photographs in the papers from time to time doing things like attending charity concerts or giving prizes. She could not remember seeing this man before in any such photographs, and yet ...

'You are wondering who I am, Mma,' the visitor said. 'You are thinking, who is this man? That is what you are thinking, is it not?'

Mma Ramotswe was momentarily taken aback. She glanced at Mma Makutsi, who was busying herself with the kettle. Mma Makutsi grinned.

'Well, yes, Rra,' Mma Ramotswe said. 'I think that I know you, but I don't, if you see what I mean. You have one of those faces ...'

'Which are very common,' said the man. 'Yes, that is true. I have a very ordinary face.'

'That is not what I was going to say, Rra,' Mma Ramotswe said quickly. 'You are a very elegant man.'

The visitor took the compliment with a nod of his head. 'My name,' he said, 'is Motalhodi Gefeli.' He paused, as if waiting for a reaction. But the name meant nothing to Mma Ramotswe, who smiled at him politely.

'Of the Gaborone Comets,' he continued.

At this, Mma Ramotswe clapped her hands together. 'Of course, Rra! Of course!'

Mr Gefeli smiled. 'I am glad to see that you

5

are a football fan, Mma,' he said. 'Some women ...' He shrugged, as if to comment on the inability of women to understand a male mystery.

'Oh, I am not a football fan,' said Mma Ramotswe. 'In fact, Rra, I know nothing about football. Nothing at all!'

Mr Gefeli raised an eyebrow. 'But you know about me?'

Mma Makutsi had made a pot of red-bush tea, and now she brought two cups on a tea tray and offered one to Mr Gefeli. 'I know about you, Rra,' she said. 'I have read all about you in the newspapers. You are the man who bought the Comets and have been making them so strong.'

Mr Gefeli accepted the cup of tea. 'You are very kind to say that, Mma,' he said. 'Yes, I am the man who bought the Comets. I am that man.'

Mma Makutsi handed the other cup of tea to Mma Ramotswe. 'Yes, and everybody,' she continued, 'is happy with what you did, because the Comets are doing so well now. You have that very good goalkeeper, don't you?'

Mma Ramotswe glanced at Mma Makutsi. This was strange. Mma Makutsi had never before expressed any interest in football, and here she was talking about a goalkeeper with none other than Mr Motalhodi Gefeli of the Gaborone Comets. She had once told Mma Makutsi that a good detective should be able to merge with his surroundings, and this involved being able to talk about the things that other people talked about. Surely the opposite effect would be achieved by a woman talking about football? Women simply did not talk about a thing like that, Mma Ramotswe reflected. But then the thought struck her: am I being old-fashioned?

'I didn't know that you were interested in football, Mma Makutsi,' she said suddenly. 'That is quite a surprise.'

For a moment, Mma Makutsi hesitated; then she smiled, a shy smile, thought Mma Ramotswe. 'I do not know a great deal about it,' she said, adding, 'but then there are some people who know even less about it than I do.' This last comment was clearly directed at Mma Ramotswe, who took it in good spirit. She knew that it was sometimes hard for Mma Makutsi, being only an assistant detective when she had gained very high marks from the Botswana Secretarial College. Mma Makutsi had achieved the previously unheard-of mark of 97 per cent in the final examinations at the college, and never hesitated to remind people of this achievement. But she should be allowed – and deserved – her little morsel of pride.

We are all proud of something, thought Mma Ramotswe. Mma Makutsi was proud of her 97 per cent. Mr J. L. B. Matekoni was proud of the fact that he had been chosen to maintain the British High Commissioner's official white vehicle. Mma Potokwani, the matron of the orphan farm, was proud of the fact that so many of the children who passed through the orphanage did well at school, found good jobs and came back to visit her with their own children. As for the two apprentices at the garage, they must be proud of something – although Mma Ramotswe found it a bit difficult to think of exactly what that might be.

Mr Gefeli was looking at Mma Makutsi with appreciation. 'Well, that is very true, Mma,' he said. 'We have that fine goalkeeper. He is called James Pikani and he is very, very good at keeping that goal. He is like a lion!' He paused, as if savouring the image. 'Yes, he is like a lion watching over the entrance to his cave.'

Like a lion, thought Mma Ramotswe. At the back of her mind there was a rather sinister story that she had heard somewhere – one of those traditional stories that grandmothers used to tell their grandchildren – about a girl who married a lion. What exactly had happened? The girl's brothers had suspected that the man who had married their sister was really a lion, and they had devised a test to see if this was true. They had been right, of course, and they had seen off their false brother-in-law, who had left lion paw marks in the sand as he ran away. Now here was this goalkeeper, James Pikani, who might really be a lion in disguise . . .

Mma Ramotswe picked up her teacup and sipped at the hot red liquid. Red-bush tea was not to everybody's liking, but it certainly was to hers, and from the way Mr Gefeli now drank his – in deep, thirsty gulps – it appeared that he approved of it too. Mma Ramotswe signalled to Mma Makutsi to refill their visitor's cup.

'This tea is very good,' said Mr Gefeli. He paused, and dabbed at his mouth with a white handkerchief that he took from the breast pocket of his suit. It was an oddly fussy gesture for a man of his build. Nor was it what one would have expected from the owner of a major football team.

Mma Ramotswe now decided that enough

time had been spent on chit-chat. It was not polite, of course, to rush straight into business, but it was equally rude to keep somebody waiting.

'Is there something you would like to talk to us about, Rra?' she asked. 'Is there something that we can do to help?'

Mr Gefeli tucked his handkerchief back into his pocket. 'Well, Mma,' he began, 'there is something. You see, I have been losing football matches.'

Mma Ramotswe sighed. She was not a sportswoman – her traditional build had always made that somewhat unlikely – but she knew enough about sports to know that somebody won, and somebody lost. There were no sports, as far as she could make out, where everybody won. If this were the case, then why should people complain if they occasionally lost?

'Somebody has to lose, Rra,' she said quietly. 'You can't have two winners. One side will win and the other will lose.'

Mr Gefeli shook his head impatiently. 'Yes, yes,' he said, 'of course I understand that. But whenever one loses, there is a reason for it. You don't lose for no reason at all. There will be some player who does not perform as well as he normally does. You will see this, and you can speak to the player and tell him where he has been going wrong. If he doesn't improve, then you can get rid of him. That is the way it's done.'

Mma Ramotswe thought about this for a moment. 'So, who is this player?' she asked. 'Who is this player who has been making you lose?'

For a moment, Mr Gefeli said nothing. He looked down at his hands, which were folded over his lap. 'James,' he muttered. 'James Pikani, our goalkeeper.'

Mma Ramotswe frowned. 'Then he isn't so good after all,' she said.

Mr Gefeli became animated. 'But he is,' he said. 'It's just that he ...' He stopped and looked at his hands again.

'Yes?' said Mma Ramotswe.

'He lets goals through,' said Mr Gefeli. 'Not all the time. Most of the time he's a brilliant goalkeeper, but then, in certain matches, he goes to pieces. I'm sure he's doing it on purpose.'

Mma Ramotswe drew in her breath sharply. Even with her scant knowledge of sports, she knew that this was the very worst thing a player could do. It was a sort of treason, she thought; the player was letting down the whole team. Of course, the reason for it was usually money.

'Somebody must be paying him,' she said. 'Don't you think that is the most likely reason, Rra?'

Mr Gefeli nodded his head. 'Yes,' he said. 'I assume that somebody is paying him, Mma. But how can I tell? How can I prove it?'

Mma Ramotswe suddenly felt more confident. This was not a matter of sport; this was a matter of simple human greed, and that was something of which she had seen a great deal. Now she was on familiar ground – the ground of the private detective.

'Would you like me to find out about this, Rra?' she said. 'Would you like me to find out whether he's getting money? I've done this sort of thing before, you know. There are ways of finding out.' Indeed there were – most of them straightforward. People who were bribed with large sums usually gave themselves away by spending those same large sums. Such people were, by nature, spenders rather than savers. Their spending was often very obvious – flashy cars, for instance.

'Yes,' said Mr Gefeli. 'I would like you to find out for me, Mma. Once I have proof, then I can act. Before that, I can do nothing – he is far too popular.'

Mma Ramotswe nodded. 'Does he drive a car?' she asked.

Mr Gefeli seemed surprised by the question. 'Yes,' he said. 'Yes, he does drive.'

'What sort of car is that?' asked Mma Ramotswe.

'An old one,' said Mr Gefeli. 'Nothing special.'

Mma Ramotswe looked disappointed. Perhaps it would not be as simple as she had thought.

2

'Well now, Mma Ramotswe,' said Mr J. L. B. Matekoni, her husband, that evening. 'You had a very important visitor this morning, didn't you?'

Mma Ramotswe did not normally discuss her clients' business. It was different, though, with Mr J. L. B. Matekoni. Although he was not exactly staff, all the same he owned Tlokweng Road Speedy Motors, in a spare room of which the No. 1 Ladies' Detective Agency had its office. This meant that he always had a fairly good idea of what was going on in the agency, even if nobody told him anything. So now Mr J. L. B. Matekoni listened closely as she told him about the problem of the Comets' goalkeeper, James Pikani, whose erratic playing had cost the team several games.

'Letting goals through?' asked Mr J. L. B. Matekoni, shaking his head in disapproval. 'That is very bad.'

Mma Ramotswe agreed. 'Money is very corrupting,' she said. 'People will do anything for money. Not everybody, of course, but some will.' As she spoke, she thought of those people who would never accept a bribe, under any circumstances, and at the head of that list, of course, was Mr J. L. B. Matekoni.

She reflected on the case that night, lying awake in her bed, waiting for sleep to come. If James Pikani was being bribed to let goals through, then there were two ways of tackling the problem. One was to find out who benefited from the resulting victory, and to try to trap them in the act of bribing, and the other was to follow the money. The first of these would be very difficult. The obvious suspect was the management of the winning team, but there was a feature which complicated the case.

In the course of their conversation earlier

that day, Mr Gefeli had made it clear that there had been several occasions on which James appeared to let goals through, and, in each case, the Comets had been playing against a different team. Why would one person want the Comets to lose a series of games, rather than just the one game in which they were playing against the briber's team? Or would it be in somebody's interest that the Comets should be less successful all round?

The more Mma Ramotswe thought about it, the more complicated it became. And the more complicated it became, the less likely it seemed to her that she would come up with a simple answer. This might take weeks, even months of investigation, and even then she might not come up with a solution.

She felt more confident the next day when she sat on her veranda shortly after sunrise, drinking her early morning cup of red-bush tea. It was her favourite time of day, a time when the world was new, when the air was sharp and fresh, with just a hint of woodsmoke from somebody's fire. She had decided that the best way to tackle this case was the way in which she tackled every case: head on.

It would be far too difficult, she felt, to find out who might be bribing the goalkeeper. So instead she would get to know James Pikani himself; that was what she would do today. She would go and see the man. She would think of a reason for visiting him, and once she found him she would rely on her greatest weapon – intuition – to work out what to do next. She would have to tread carefully, of course; one could hardly ask him outright whether he was being bribed. But there were ways of finding these things out. You could find out whether somebody was honest or not by watching his or her eyes. It was not difficult.

In the office that morning, as she and Mma Makutsi were dealing with the day's post, Mma Ramotswe asked her assistant what she knew about James. 'You're the one who seems to know everything about football,' she began. 'At least, you knew all about this James Pikani. Or so you said.'

'I did not say that I knew everything,' corrected Mma Makutsi. 'I just said that I knew that he was the goalkeeper. I know a girl who was his girlfriend once. That is how I knew.'

Mma Ramotswe leaned forward. This remark of Mma Makutsi's, this casual reference to a girlfriend, was a possible way in to the meeting that she needed with the footballer.

'This girlfriend, Mma,' she said. 'Who is she?'

Mma Makutsi adjusted her spectacles – the large, round spectacles that she wore. She enjoyed imparting knowledge, and she did so with the air of a schoolteacher spelling out the obvious to a class of none-too-bright pupils. 'She is called Alice,' she replied. 'She works in a shoe shop in town. It is a very good shop, and they brought in these new shoes the other day. You should have seen them, Mma Ramotswe, they were—'

'Yes, yes,' interrupted Mma Ramotswe. Mma Makutsi's weakness for fashionable shoes was well known, and she could talk for hours on the subject. 'But this Alice – what has she said about James? Has she told you much about him?'

Mma Makutsi looked out of the window. 'A little,' she said. She paused. 'Very little, in fact. She said that he comes from Lobatse.' She paused. 'She said that he was not a good boyfriend, and that she was pleased when she got rid of him. Just a little sad, maybe. You know how it is when a man goes away. You feel a bit sad, and then you get better.'

Mma Ramotswe nodded. 'Is that all she said about him – that he came from Lobatse?'

Mma Makutsi thought for a moment. 'I think so,' she said.

'Do you think you could find out anything else, Mma?' she asked. 'Could you phone Alice and ask her?'

Mma Makutsi nodded. 'She likes to talk,' she said. 'I don't think that she would mind being phoned at work.'

While Mma Makutsi dialled the number of the shoe shop, Mma Ramotswe busied herself with pen and paper. At the top of a page she wrote: *James Pikani*, and underneath that she wrote: *Comes from Lobatse; had girlfriend called Alice; drives old car (according to Mr Gefeli)*. That, she thought, is all we know about him, apart from the fact that he is a very fine goalkeeper (sometimes).

Mma Ramotswe tried to make sense of what was said on the phone between Mma Makutsi and Alice, but it was difficult to reconstruct the conversation when she could only hear one side of it. There were plenty of ahs and ohs from Mma Makutsi and at one point a sharp intake of breath, but that was all. It was clear, though, that a good deal of information was being gathered.

'Well?' she said to her assistant at the end of the call. 'What did she say?'

'Nothing much,' said Mma Makutsi airily. 'Most of the time she was talking about his brother, whom Alice has her eye on. He's quite a ladies' man, it would seem.'

'And James?' asked Mma Ramotswe. 'What about James?'

Mma Makutsi shrugged. 'All she said was that he was very vain. She said that he was the vainest man she had ever met. He always looked at himself in mirrors. Even in the car he would look at himself in the mirror, just to check that he was still handsome.'

Mma Ramotswe sighed. It was not very much information to go on. Many men were vain these days, she thought. It was something to do with women being free to look at men in the same way in which men had always looked at women. Women had not realised it, but all that this new freedom led to was the creation of a lot of vain men.

She wrote down the word *vain* on her sheet of paper and then put it to one side, tucked into a file that she had opened under James Pikani's name. The post had brought one or two letters to be answered, and she decided that she would attend to these now, dictating her responses to Mma Makutsi. Later on, she would come back to the question of how she might find out more about James Pikani before she sought him out.

She finished dictating the letters by the mid-morning tea break. It was a fine morning, not too hot, and she thought that she would drink her tea with Mr J. L. B. Matekoni and his two apprentices. They liked to sit at the side of the garage and have their tea there, and it was an ideal spot on a day like this.

Her teacup in hand, Mma Ramotswe surveyed the scene. Mr J. L. B. Matekoni was sitting, legs stretched out, on an old car seat that he had placed against the garage wall, while the two apprentices were perched on top of two upturned oil drums. Mma Ramotswe joined them, lowering herself on to a box which she used as a seat when she took her tea with the mechanics.

She looked at Charlie, the elder of the two apprentices. He was looking up into the sky, smiling at something, and she wondered what it was. Probably some football victory, she imagined ... Then a thought occurred to her.

'Charlie,' she said, 'have you heard of a goalkeeper called James Pikani?'

His daydream interrupted, Charlie looked at Mma Ramotswe in surprise. 'Of course I have,' he said. 'Everybody knows James. He's a really good player. Although recently he's been useless. Maybe he's getting too old. Maybe he's lost interest.'

'He's finished,' chipped in the younger apprentice. 'The crowd sometimes gets angry with him, you know. They call out rude names. They shout that he's an old man, that he needs glasses or that he's forgotten how to play. They make it very tough for him.'

Mma Ramotswe had been half listening to what the younger apprentice had been saying. Now she stood up, spilling some of her tea as she did so.

'Are you going somewhere?' Mr J. L. B. Matekoni asked. 'You haven't finished your tea.'

Mma Ramotswe made a vague gesture with her free hand. 'I have to go out,' she said. 'There is somebody I need to speak to.'

Inside the office, she found Mma Makutsi still drinking her tea, paging through a fashion magazine; the magazine was open at a page where people were showing off shoes. It was just the sort of thing, Mma Ramotswe thought, which Mma Makutsi would find fascinating.

'Mma Makutsi,' she said. 'Would you like to come with me to have a word with James Pikani?'

Mma Makutsi needed no persuading, and soon she and Mma Ramotswe were on their way together in the tiny white van. They followed the road that led to the address which Mr Gefeli had given them the day before, to the house occupied by Mr James Pikani. It was not, she noted, a fashionable address. It was a small plot on the edge of Old Naledi, a house that would never have suggested itself as the house of a famous footballer, let alone one who was being bribed with a great deal of money.

A middle-aged woman opened the door when Mma Ramotswe knocked. She stared at her two visitors for a moment, and then greeted them politely in the traditional way.

'I'm sorry to bother you, Mma,' said Mma Ramotswe. 'You must be the mother of James. He is the person we would like to speak to.'

The woman nodded. 'This is his house,' she said, 'and I am his mother.' She paused, as if wondering whether she should let two strangers in to see her son. 'He is resting now. Is it important?'

Mma Ramotswe did not hesitate. 'It is very important,' she said.

The woman nodded. 'You should come in, please,' she said, gesturing for them to follow her. 'You can sit here, and I shall call him.'

They sat in the small parlour, which also served as a dining room and kitchen. Mma Ramotswe looked about her, as she always did when entering an unfamiliar room. She noticed the calendar stuck on the wall, advertising football boots; she noticed the rickety display cabinet with the school sporting trophies neatly arranged along the shelves; she noticed the old photograph of a boy in scout uniform having a badge pinned on his chest. She saw some other things, and everything she saw told her: this is not the house of a man who would take a bribe.

After a few minutes, James Pikani appeared. He looked as if he had been asleep, as his eyes were puffy and the T-shirt he was wearing was crumpled. Mma Ramotswe rose to her feet and greeted him. Then she introduced him to Mma Makutsi who, struck by the presence of a famous person, couldn't help doing a little curtsey.

'What can I do for you, ladies?' asked James Pikani.

Mma Ramotswe looked embarrassed. 'Just your autograph, Rra,' she said. 'That would be enough.'

James Pikani laughed. 'Oh, is that all? Well, of course, we need to keep the fans happy!'

'That is very kind of you, Rra,' said Mma Ramotswe. 'I've brought a little book for you to sign in, and a pencil, too.'

She held out a small black book, which he took from her. Then she fished into the bag she had with her and took out a pencil.

'Here, Rra,' she said. 'Catch.'

With that, she threw the pencil towards James Pikani. The footballer reached out, but his hand was nowhere near the pencil and it dropped to the floor.

'I'm sorry, Rra,' said Mma Ramotswe, as she stooped to retrieve the pencil. 'Here it is.'

3

She telephoned Mr Gefeli later that day and invited him to come to the office. She had important news for him, she said.

'You have solved the case?' he asked. 'You have solved it so quickly?'

'Yes,' said Mma Ramotswe. 'Come in to the office and I will tell you all about it.'

Mr Gefeli arrived quickly. As he sat with a cup of red-bush tea in front of him, Mma Ramotswe gave him the good news.

'Your goalkeeper,' she announced, 'is not corrupt.'

Mr Gefeli looked doubtful. 'Are you sure about that, Mma?'

Mma Ramotswe smiled. 'I am very sure,' she said. 'He is not corrupt – just short-sighted.'

Mr Gefeli looked blank. 'I do not understand,' he began.

'Male vanity,' said Mma Ramotswe. 'Here we have a sporting hero who is very vain. He realises that he needs glasses, but he is too vain to wear them. He does nothing, in the hope that the problem will go away. It doesn't.' Mma Ramotswe paused as her explanation sank in. 'So all you have to do is to have a word with him,' she said. 'Persuade him to go to the optician.'

Mr Gefeli scratched his head. 'This is a very strange outcome,' he said. 'I had no idea.' He stared at Mma Ramotswe in wonderment. 'Please tell me, Mma. How did you find this out?'

'It was simple,' said Mma Ramotswe. 'I listened, and I looked. Something one of those apprentices said made me think. Once I had thought, I acted.'

'What did you do?' asked Mr Gefeli.

'I threw a pencil at him,' said Mma Ramotswe, 'and he didn't catch it.'

It took Mr Gefeli a few moments to work out what had happened. Then he realised, and his face broke into a broad smile.

'You are a very clever lady, Mma Ramotswe,' he said.

'Thank you, Rra,' said Mma Ramotswe. 'And now – more tea?'

A High Wind in Nevis

Marlin House sits on top of a hill above an old port on the Caribbean island of Nevis. It was built in the late 1950s by a retired doctor, who wanted a retreat on that part of the island and who enjoyed giving parties. A celebrated American writer would come to these parties, when he was in residence at his luxurious villa further up the coast, along with other well-known and glamorous people who were passing through. The doctor was a generous host, and the maker of a legendary rum punch.

When the doctor died, his son ignored the place, and the house fell into disrepair. The thick, jungle-like vegetation that covered the hillside was meant to be kept in check by a gardener, but this gardener's sight was bad and became steadily worse. Either he did not see the creepers that were beginning to cover the terrace, or he had given up what must have been an unequal battle. Plants grew quickly there. Then there were the high winds – 'the breeze' as the locals called it – which tore down trees and branches, and the rains – the warm, pelting rain that clogged the storm drains.

When the house was eventually put up for sale, it attracted the attention of a couple who happened to be motoring along the coast road in an old Volkswagen car. The man, a small, rather insignificant-looking person, was Dutch. The woman, who was taller and more powerfully built, was from Trinidad and of mixed ancestry.

They had met in a club in Miami, the Blue Cocktail, and decided to cast their lot in with each other. Marcus, the Dutchman, had spent ten years as a schoolteacher on the island of Curaçao, and wanted to stay in the Caribbean. Georgina, the Trinidadian, was undecided about returning, but she wanted to travel with Marcus. Now, rather against her will, she was falling in love again with a world that she had not very long ago left with such eagerness.

They had seen the retired doctor's house from the road below, from where they could just make out the top of its roof. On impulse, Georgina, at the wheel of the old Volkswagen, had turned up the narrow, potholed track that led up the hillside.

'You never know,' she said. 'When we get to the top we might see a For Sale sign.'

'And?' asked Marcus.

'And then we buy it and turn it into a hotel,' said Georgina abruptly. 'What else?'

Georgina had a vaguely angry way of talking, as if challenging the person to whom she was speaking to argue with her. This manner, Marcus had discovered, did not conceal a sweet personality – in fact, she was by nature irritable. But he was smitten, and would hear nothing against her. 'My ever-so-slightly angry Georgina,' he said to her. Georgina snapped back, 'What exactly do you mean by that?'

They had to drive slowly up the track, and at one point Marcus had to get out of the car and attempt to move a tree branch that had fallen and blocked the road. Georgina remained in the car, tapping the steering wheel with her fingers as she watched her friend's futile efforts. Eventually, after several fruitless minutes, she got out of the car, lifted up the branch and shifted it to the side of the road.

'You're truly magnificent,' said Marcus.

'And you're truly weak,' said Georgina, getting back into the car.

They drove on. There, on the rusted ironwork gate at the foot of the drive that led to Marlin House, was a sign that said 'For Sale'. They parked the Volkswagen and walked up the drive. A pair of birds of prey circled overhead on the currents of wind from the headland; the fronds of great coconut palms moved like fans against the sky.

'Our hotel,' said Georgina.

The hotel opened its doors three months later. The house, rescued from ruin just in time, had been renewed from floor to ceiling. Georgina oversaw all of the work, criticising the carpenters, scolding the upholsterers, snapping at the electrician. Marcus looked after the kitchen: ordering pots and pans and catering ovens, planning recipes, and contacting suppliers of eggs and vegetables.

'That bossy woman,' complained one of the carpenters to a friend. 'She too much trouble, man. One day a coconut go fall on her head!'

'Even the Lord, he frighten' of her,' said another. 'People come stay in that place, they see her, they run fast, jump in sea.'

When everything was ready, or slightly before, the guests started to arrive. They were generally enchanted with their lodgings. The view from the terrace, over the treetops to a sea of an impossible blue, took their breath away. Guests sat there, their feet up on the terrace parapet, the warm breeze in their hair, sipping at the rum cocktails which the barman brought on a silver tray. They walked down to the beach and swam in the breakers; they watched the highly coloured fishing boats, painted in bright blues and greens, nose out into the waves and then, in the evenings, Marcus's carefully planned dinners rounded off the day. Everything seemed perfect, from the guests' point of view, except for the management.

The running of a hotel inevitably brings requests from the guests. Nothing is ever quite right for everybody: one guest will want a larger towel; another will wonder why there is no fridge in the room; and so on. The usual hotel owners will listen to these complaints and make an effort to deal with the problem. Larger towels may be found, or at least promised. Fridges can be held out as a possibility, even if realistically they are not. The important thing, as any hotelier will tell you, is that the guest should feel that their request is a reasonable one and that something will be done to attend to it.

But at Marlin House it was different. 'What do you need a fridge for?' was Georgina's response to a guest who liked the idea of keeping a supply of cold milk in the room.

'Because the milk curdles so quickly in this

heat. It would be nice to make tea in the room.'

'Plenty of milk in the kitchen. Go ask for it there.'

'Well, could we at least have some biscuits in the room? To snack on?'

'Food in the rooms brings cockroaches.'

Georgina's fierce reputation grew. 'A delightful setting,' wrote one travel writer, 'which is well worth a visit if you are in that part of the Caribbean. The rooms are comfortable and the Caribbean-style cuisine delicious. But do not engage with the management on any issue.'

Such comments served only to fuel curiosity, and people started to choose the hotel in order to experience at first hand Georgina's highly individual style. Usually they were not disappointed. In fact, they delighted in the disgrace into which an inappropriate request or suggestion cast them. The hotel was becoming legendary.

Georgina's famous look of disapproval could be imitated over the dinner table but never equalled. Her thunderous expression when a female guest was unwise enough to ask Marcus, in the middle of a party, to dance with her was talked about for months.

At the end of their first five years in the

hotel, Marcus and Georgina decided to hold a New Year's Eve party to celebrate the success of the hotel and the new year itself. Word got out, and it was not long before all the rooms were taken for the new year holiday. Reviewing their bookings, Marcus smiled with pleasure at the thought of what this would do for the hotel's finances, but Georgina frowned. Although she never admitted it to Marcus, guests annoyed her. They were so needy, so helpless. They made stupidly fussy requests. They never seemed pleased with what you gave them. Their conversation was so dull, their questions so childish.

'If I'm asked again about those humming birds, I shall scream,' she said one day. To the next guest who asked her, 'What are those lovely little birds with their long tails? The ones that hover in front of the flowers? Look, there's one now!', she replied, 'Small vultures,' and turned on her heel.

'That was rather unkind,' said Marcus, who had witnessed the incident.

'Don't talk to me about it,' said Georgina, with her discouraging face which was so much part of her character. 'Just don't.'

The New Year's Eve party was attended not only by the resident guests, but by people from the area. Some guests remembered the retired doctor, his parties, and the American writer who came to them. 'He would have loved this,' they said. 'He loved a party.'

'Frightful man,' said Georgina.

'Oh, did you ever meet him?'

'Certainly not.'

They had brought in a three-piece band from the town, and the musicians played on the terrace while people stood at the parapet and looked down at the lights of the town and, beyond the town, to the sea. It was a windy night, but the air was warm and scented with the flowers that grew in the windward section of the garden. Down in the darkness below, from time to time somebody would send up a firework rocket that would break into a cone of falling stars, and the people on the terrace would clap or whistle in admiration.

As the old year faded into the new, champagne was opened and the guests broke into a rendition of 'Auld Lang Syne', linking hands and stepping backwards and forwards on the creaky planks of the terrace. Georgina sat to one side. She looked disapproving for some reason, as if the ending of the old year was a personal affront or a private loss.

Then she went out, by herself, glass in hand,

and stood on the lawn under one of the swaying coconut trees. Marcus saw her from the terrace and called out, but his voice was swallowed by a strong gust of wind. It was the same gust of wind that dislodged a large coconut, which fell directly on Georgina's head.

There was a shout from the terrace. 'Georgina's down ...' Then a rush as the guests made their way to the lawn. Georgina lay there, unconscious. A nurse among the guests reached down and took her pulse. 'She's been knocked out,' she said. 'Get her inside.'

They put her to bed while they telephoned for an ambulance. Nobody answered at the other end, and so they tried the number of a local doctor. He said, 'I've been at a party. I'm not sure if I can drive ...' But he agreed to come, and when he arrived two hours later, with a small cut on his face that nobody asked about, Georgina had already come round.

'I hope everyone enjoyed themselves,' she said. 'I would not like to think that I had spoiled the party.'

Marcus looked at her in surprise. His surprise continued the next morning when Georgina, back on her feet, went round the hotel wishing everybody a happy new year and asking them whether there was anything she could do for them.

'Somebody's made a new year's resolution,' muttered one of the guests. 'It won't last.'

Marcus was astonished at the change in Georgina's character. 'She's not the same any more,' he said. 'Georgina used to be so forceful, so ... well, so firm. Now she's ... well, a bit ... well, you know what I mean.'

It continued like that for at least a month. Then one morning Georgina came back from a short walk in the neighbouring coconut grove. She snapped at the chef and immediately after that was very sharp with one of the guests, who had told her that his coffee was cold.

Overhearing this, Marcus felt his heart leap with pleasure. She's back, he thought. My ever-so-slightly irritable Georgina is back!

He looked out of the window. The wind, that warm wind from the west, had started again, making the coconut palms sway backwards and forwards against the sky, gently, but enough to dislodge the fruit, sending it earthwards.

Fabrizia

Fabrizia could not remember her mother very well. In fact, she was worried that such memories as she had, vague and ill-defined ones, were of the wrong person, and that the woman she was thinking of was actually an aunt who had left Italy to live in the United States and never returned.

'Four is not too early to remember,' said her father, Alessio. 'Many people remember being four quite well. I do, for one. I remember travelling on the train all the way from Reggio Emilia to Milan and seeing a man with one leg standing near the entrance, begging. I remember that, you know. I think that you'll be able to remember your mother if you try.'

She had tried, and had told her father that she remembered something – a beautiful woman with a smell of flowery soap, and he had said, 'Yes! Yes! That's her, my darling, that's your mother.'

But she had seen a picture of the aunt, and the face in the picture and the face in the memory seemed to her to be one and the same person. She did not mention this to her father, though, because he was desperate that she should have a memory of her mother, his wife, who had died so unexpectedly and left him to raise their daughter. They had been a small family, just the two of them, but it did not matter. He lived for her, and told his friends that he would have died for her, willingly, several times over if necessary, to protect her from the dangers of the world.

'Look what's happened to Italy,' he said. 'All this lawlessness. I remember when this was the safest place in the world to be. Nothing ever happened in those days. Nothing.'

He was well off by the standards of Reggio Emilia, the town in which they lived. There was great wealth in Milan and Bologna, of course, and Parma too, with all its elegance. Reggio Emilia was much simpler than its well-known neighbours, but there was money to be made there too, and he had done well with the two shops that he owned in the centre of the town, in a street that led off the Piazza Cavour. One of these shops sold furniture and carpets, and the other was a dress shop that specialised in clothing for short, fat ladies.

'Now that we have so many Southerners up

here,' Alessio said to a friend, 'there will be a big demand for dresses to fit squat ladies. That is the shape they are, these women from Naples and Sicily. Look at them.'

His friend thought about this. He was probably right; people from the south of Italy tended to be shorter than those from the north, but that was due to diet, was it not? Once they moved to the north, to take up jobs in prosperous towns like Reggio or Modena, their children would grow to be much taller. A good diet could make all the difference. It was diet, not genes.

Alessio did not believe this. He had a deep prejudice against people from the south, whom he believed to be responsible for all of Italy's woes.

'Look at Naples,' he said. 'Look at the proportion of the population down there who are involved in criminal activities. Do you know what it is? I'll tell you: thirty per cent.'

'Surely not?' said his friend. 'Surely not one in three people.'

'Amazing, isn't it?' said Alessio. 'Just think of it. Every third person in Naples makes his living from crime.'

Whatever his prejudices against Southerners might have been, Alessio got on well with the customers who came into his clothes shop. The squat ladies who came to buy outfits for weddings and christenings were also cheerful and polite, and he even found himself enjoying the company of the Southern assistants whom he had taken on. These girls were all involved with young men, whom they spoke about endlessly. The young men had names like Salvatore or Pasquale – 'Typical names from Naples,' muttered Alessio. 'Look at the names in the newspaper reports of the trials in the criminal courts. Salvatore this, Salvatore that. They're the ones who commit all the crimes in this country. Typical!'

Fabrizia was used to these views from her father. She had heard them all her life – but did not agree with them. She rather liked Southerners; she liked the way they talked, and she liked Southern cuisine. She had heard about corruption and the Mafia and the ongoing economic problems of the Mezzogiorno, as Italians called the south, but these did not interest her very much. 'Nobody's perfect,' she said to her father. 'There's been corruption even in the Vatican, hasn't there? No, don't shake your head like that. What about your precious Christian Democrats? When they were in power what did you have? Honesty? Hah!'

Alessio did not mind hearing these views expressed by his daughter. He shrugged his shoulders. 'I don't care what your political views turn out to be, just as long as you don't marry one of those people. That's all. Don't end up marrying a man from Naples, a Neapolitan. I couldn't bear that. I really couldn't.'

At the age of twenty-three, when Fabrizia had finished her course at the University of Parma, she came home to help Alessio with his shops. She proved to have a good head for business, and within two years they had acquired a further three shops. These shops also sold clothes: one specialised in teenage clothing, and played loud music at its entrance; one stocked children's outfits and the third sold clothing for work – waiters' outfits, maids' skirts and the like. All of these businesses thrived, and Alessio and Fabrizia became more and more wealthy.

Then one evening Alessio happened to see his daughter in a restaurant. It was not a restaurant that he was used to visiting, and both he and Fabrizia were surprised to see one another there. He, in particular, was taken aback by the fact that she had a young man with her.

The young man stood up politely when Alessio approached the table, and the older man knew immediately. The young man was a Southerner, a Neapolitan, no doubt. He could tell. He had never been wrong about things like that.

Alessio stared at the gold chain around the young man's neck, and the small charm it bore that was supposed to ward off the evil eye, a tiny gold *cornicello*, or horn. This would never be worn by anybody from the north, where belief in such things was looked down upon; Northerners, in his view, had no time for such superstitions – and quite rightly too.

There was a tense exchange of words between the two men, about nothing in particular. The young man was called Salvatore, and he had intense green eyes, which he focused on Alessio. The older man, however, could not bring himself to return this frank stare. He looked at his daughter instead, almost begging, as if to say to her, 'Please tell me that this young man is nothing to you, a casual friend.' But of course the look that she gave her father implied the opposite, and he knew then, with complete certainty, that this young man was to be his son-in-law.

He was not surprised, therefore, when

Fabrizia came to him three weeks later and announced that she wished to marry Salvatore.

'I know what your views are about people like him,' she said. 'No, don't try to deny it, Father. You don't like Southerners. You just don't. It's so unfair on people like Salvatore.'

Alessio looked down at the ground. He could hardly deny the truth of her words; after all, he had never hesitated to express his views to her, even when she was a child. He had impressed upon her, time and again, the need to distrust those from the south. In fact, he had tried without shame to shape her views – and now she had reacted by choosing to marry a Southerner. It had been a bad mistake on his part. One cannot tell one's children what to think, he had read; try to do that, and you'll lose them. They'll do the opposite – the exact opposite – of what you want them to do. Be careful. He had paid no attention to this advice, and this was the result.

He looked up at his daughter. You are so dear to me, he thought; you are my world. You and my shops – our little world.

She looked back at him. I didn't choose him just because he's a Southerner, she thought. You imagine that I did, but it's not that. I love this man. Where he's from is nothing to do with it. Nothing.

43

They did not say a word. After a few minutes, she sighed and rose to her feet. Leaving the room, she glanced back at her father briefly and shook her head, as if in judgement. For a moment his heart stopped from fear at the thought of losing her, but then he said to himself, I shall fight back, because if you don't fight for what you have, for what you've worked for, then some Southerner is going to come along and take it away from you. The thought gave him comfort, and he stared at her defiantly as she left the room. *All right! Marry him, and see what it's like.*

Both father and daughter made an effort at the wedding. Alessio hired a hotel in the hills and paid for a lavish meal. He sat through the ceremony with a fixed smile, and kept this smile in place at the reception. He was seated between two of Salvatore's aunts, both of whom conformed to his vision of Southern middle-aged women. They were widows who had been married to men who had no doubt worn ill-fitting dark suits and old-fashioned black felt hats. There were many of these widows in the south, he reflected, because the men died young. Why did they die? It was because of violence and bad driving and impatience.

44

At the end of the reception, when the couple was due to go away, he stood awkwardly by the door of the hotel while the aunts fussed round and friends said goodbye to Fabrizia, girls he had known as his daughter's childhood friends, adults now, themselves married or destined for marriage. He looked at these young women with a fond eye and remembered them as girls all those years ago, when they came to the house to see Fabrizia. Childhood was so brief, so fleeting: we have our children for so short a time. He felt the tears in his eyes and he fought them back. His fixed smile returned.

Then, just before they left, Alessio's new son-in-law Salvatore came up to him and stood before him, holding out his hand. Alessio took the younger man's hand, but avoided his gaze.

'I know you don't approve of me,' Salvatore said to him, his voice lowered. 'I can tell that. But I promise you I'll look after your daughter. I give you my word as ...' He stopped, and although Alessio waited for him to finish the sentence, he did not.

He looked at the young man. 'Thank you,' he said. 'You can tell how a father feels, can't you?'

'Yes,' said Salvatore. 'That is why I'm asking you to trust me.'

Alessio closed his eyes. 'I shall try,' he said.

Salvatore pressed his hand, and then dropped it. There was laughter from a group of Fabrizia's friends – a final joke before the couple moved through the door, beneath the flashing of cameras, and into the car which had been brought up to the front of the hotel and which Salvatore's brothers were now showering with confetti.

They had never formally discussed Salvatore's entry into the business, but Fabrizia brought him in anyway, and Alessio did not challenge her. After a while Alessio would have agreed, had his daughter ever asked him, that his new son-in-law was a remarkable salesman. The takings of the shop which he supervised went up noticeably, and Alessio himself asked Salvatore to come and apply these skills in the other shops, which went on to see an improvement too.

The warmth that had grown in their working relationship now came into their personal lives. Alessio went for dinner with Fabrizia and Salvatore and bought them expensive gifts for the house. Salvatore returned these favours, inviting his father-in-law to join them at a restaurant he liked, where he introduced him to the proprietor – a Southerner from Naples – with pride. He bought Alessio a new briefcase, made of supple leather from Florence, and had his initials engraved on the flap in handsome gold lettering.

Fabrizia was pleased by this flowering of friendship, and over the months that followed the wedding she and her father returned to their earlier closeness. Alessio even permitted himself to make a remark about grandchildren, and how he felt 'just about ready' for a grandson. As he said this, he thought *even if he ends up being called Pasquale*, but he did not say this, of course; he just smiled at the idea.

Then he noticed one morning that Fabrizia seemed upset about something. She was moody and snapped at a customer, which was something for which he would normally have told her off. But now he held back. Something was wrong.

Fabrizia's mood seemed to pass, but a few days later he came upon her sitting in her office, her head sunk in her hands.

'There's something wrong,' he said, resting his hand on her shoulder. 'I can tell. There's something wrong.'

She did not look up. She was silent.

'You can confide in your father, surely?' he

said. The thought occurred to him, with a sudden feeling of dread, that she was having difficulty becoming pregnant. Perhaps there was not going to be a grandson after all?

He wanted to say something reassuring to her but he could not find the words, and so he remained silent, as did she. But he felt, through his hand upon her shoulder, that she was sobbing, quietly and privately.

Salvatore seemed unchanged. Perhaps it is easier for a man to come to terms with this, thought Alessio. Or perhaps he is just braver; and his admiration for his son-in-law increased. He now found himself embarrassed by the memory of his earlier opposition to Salvatore, and marvelled at the young man's ability to rise above it, to forgive him for his barely hidden hostility.

Then one evening Fabrizia came to Alessio's house. She let herself in with her key and found her father in his sitting room, his feet up on the leather footstool in the shape of a pig which his wife had found for him and which was one of his favourite mementos of her.

Fabrizia stared at him, but her mind seemed to be elsewhere.

'Salvatore . . .' she began.

'Yes?'

'He's seeing other women,' she said, and then she began to sob.

He stood up and placed his arm around her.

'Surely not?' he said. 'Surely you're imagining this?'

'He is,' she sobbed, shaking her head. 'He is. A wife knows.'

He stroked her hair gently. 'But have you any proof? Have you?'

It became clear that she did not, and he told her, in a reassuring tone, that she should not assume that just because some Southern men carried on with other women Salvatore would do the same. 'He is a fine boy,' he said. 'I can tell. I can judge the character of men. I know that he is a good husband to you.'

She stared at him. 'But you ...'

'You should not judge a man on the basis of where he comes from,' he said. 'Forget about this. A suspicious wife can drive a man into the arms of another woman. I've seen it happen.'

Over the next few weeks, nothing more was said on the subject. Alessio began gently to raise it with his daughter on one occasion, but her look made it clear that she did not wish to discuss it. Then, on a Saturday morning, when they were both working in one of the shops, Salvatore drew up at the front door in an expensive new car. It was a surprise to both of them, and they went out to inspect it. Salvatore smiled and gestured proudly at the gleaming bodywork.

Alessio reflected, later, on what a car such as that must have cost. It was family money, perhaps; there was a wealthy uncle somewhere down there, he had heard. But Fabrizia had different views.

'Can't you see?' she said to her father. 'He's stealing the money from the business. He's stealing the money from *you*!'

He was shocked by the suggestion and turned on her, accusing her of being unfair to her husband, betraying him. 'Don't imagine that everybody from down there is dishonest,' he stormed. 'Don't make that mistake.'

She looked at him open-mouthed. '*I* should not make that mistake?' she said. '*I*?'

But Alessio had walked off, dismissing his daughter with a wave of his hand. Fabrizia stood quite still, and then shrugged. She muttered something, but he did not hear what she said, and he was not interested.

Two days later, Salvatore drove off in the expensive car, a young woman in the passenger seat beside him. He was heading south. The husband of one of Fabrizia's friends, a police officer, saw him as he drove out of town, and told them about it. Fabrizia immediately checked the main business bank account – an account to which Salvatore had been given free access. It had been emptied.

She went into her father's office.

'My dear,' he sighed. 'I'm so sorry. I tried to warn you, didn't I? I really tried.'

Namaqualand Daisies

1

He was called the Captain, although he did not like the title and had asked people not to use the rank to which he had been briefly entitled because of his service in Hong Kong. That had been in China, and was back then. This was Africa, and this was now, 1956, and he was a plain district officer in Basutoland – nothing special. Just ordinary Mr Andrews. But someone had seen the letter addressed to him as Captain, and it had got about that this was what he was. In colonial society, particularly one tucked away in a mountain kingdom, anything that suggested a rank or a title was welcome. Such places were full of wartime majors and the like, hanging on to what remained of their authority and importance. The Captain was far too young for that; he was barely thirty-five, and his wife was even younger. She had laughed when she first heard him addressed as Captain.

'It makes you sound like one of those old salts,' she said. 'It makes you sound ridiculous.'

'I didn't ask anybody to call me that,' said the Captain. 'It's like a nickname, you know. You can't stop people from calling you by a nickname. You just can't.'

2

The Captain's wife did not like the country. She had tried to create a garden in the grounds of their house in Maseru, but had been defeated. There were white ants that ate the fruit trees she planted; there was not enough rain; the sun was too hot.

'I don't know if I'm going to be able to stick this out,' she wrote to a friend. 'This place is so far from everywhere. South Africa is just over the border, but you have to travel for miles and miles before you come across anybody who speaks English. They're all so insular. So petty.'

Her friend wrote back: 'Darling, you sound awful. What you must ask yourself is this: are you prepared to throw your life away for Hugh's sake? I know that he's frightfully good-looking and, well, I can understand that side of things, but are you sure? Are you really sure?'

Of course, once she asked herself whether she was sure, she realised that she was not. She was bored with their life. She was bored with this life where she knew every face she was likely ever to meet, and where there was nobody who had anything new to say.

She looked at the Captain and thought: I don't want to hurt him. He's a kind man. But I can't bear this any longer.

The Captain, gazing back at his wife – the wife he feared he barely knew – understood what she was thinking and realised then that he had lost her.

3

After his wife had gone, several people took pity on the Captain. There was the widow of a Scottish cattle-trader, a woman who had been in the country for thirty years and who spoke fluent Sesotho. There was the wife of the judge, a woman who moved in a cloud of scent and cultivated large beds of Namaqualand daisies in her garden. These women, particularly the cattle-trader's widow, invited the Captain to dinner once or twice a week.

'Poor man,' said the judge's wife. 'That young woman was obviously never going to cope with the life here. People like her shouldn't marry men like the Captain. She should have stayed in Suffolk, or wherever it was that she came from.'

'She had a roving eye,' said the cattle-trader's widow.

The judge's wife seemed surprised. 'Oh? How could you tell?'

'I just could,' said the cattle-trader's widow. 'I find that I can always tell. I'm very rarely wrong about these things.'

They invited the Captain to play bridge twice a week. He usually partnered the cattle-trader's widow, and the judge's wife played opposite her husband, a man of few words who always seemed to be staring off into the distance, even when the cards were in his hand. People said that this was because he was unhappy in his job, and that he thought of the men he was obliged to sentence to prison.

'He's too sensitive for the work he does,' said the cattle-trader's widow. 'An empire is a brutal thing, you know. I remember my husband saying that. Brutal.'

4

The Captain received a visit from a boy, who was a cousin of his wife. This boy was eighteen and was wandering around before he went to university. He wrote to the Captain and asked him whether he could stay for a few weeks. His ship was due to arrive in Cape Town, and he would come up from there to Basutoland straight away.

The Captain was pleased to discover that the boy was a good cricketer. The cricket team in which the Captain played was in need of a bowler, and the boy fitted the bill perfectly. During the day, the boy went to a local school and taught cricket there. This was done at the suggestion of the Captain, who thought that it was better for the boy to be doing something rather than sitting about the house all day.

He took the boy with him on a trip down to the south of the country when he had to visit his junior administrators. They went into the mountains on Basuto ponies and set up camp near a small river, which tumbled down the hillside. From this camp the night was a dark blanket under a sky that was filled with sparkling constellations of stars. It made one dizzy to lie back and look up into the heavens. 'That way,' said the Captain, 'that way, down there, is the Indian Ocean.'

'I know,' said the boy.

5

After the boy had stayed for three months, the Captain said to him that it was time to consider moving on. The boy held the Captain's gaze for a few moments, then looked away, in the direction of the hills. 'I don't think so,' he said. 'Not just yet. I'm helping that cricket team to improve. I'd like to stay longer. I take it that's all right with you.'

It was not a question, it was a statement. The Captain opened his mouth to say something, but stopped when he saw the boy staring at him. He turned away in silence.

Some days later, the judge's wife gave a party. The boy arrived late; nobody was sure if he had been invited. There was whisky available, and many of the guests drank more than was wise. At one point in the evening, the boy was seen talking to the cattle-trader's widow. The boy said something and then leaned forward and whispered in her ear. She recoiled sharply and then – although few people saw this – she slapped the boy across the face and walked away. The Captain did not witness this incident; nor did the judge's wife. The judge saw it, though, looking over the top of his whisky glass. He frowned and turned away, staring up at the veranda ceiling, as he often did when they played bridge out there because of the heat.

The cattle-trader's widow did not speak to the Captain about what had happened at the party. But she was worried; she was very fond of the Captain's company, and she would be devastated if there were any scandal and the Captain were obliged to go away. It would be the end of her world, she thought. No more bridge. No more dinner parties. It would be the end of everything.

The judge's wife spoke directly. 'There's something going on,' she said. 'That boy is blackmailing the Captain. It's pretty obvious, wouldn't you say?'

'We need to get rid of him,' said the cattle-trader's widow.

The judge's wife, who had been looking out of the window at her beds of Namaqualand daisies, turned round sharply. 'But he's refused to go,' she said.

6

They all played bridge the following Thursday. The Captain arrived late – they always started at seven-thirty, after dinner, and he did not arrive until a quarter to eight. They saw the lights of his car sweep across the wall as he swung round the curve of the drive.

'That'll be the Captain,' said the judge's wife. 'He's normally so punctual.'

The bridge game started. The Captain and the cattle-trader's widow held all the strong cards, it seemed, but the Captain was quiet.

The judge's wife asked after the boy. Was he still teaching cricket at the school? 'No,' said the Captain. 'He's gone.'

The judge looked up from his cards. 'Probably about time,' he muttered. 'How long had he been staying with you?'

The judge's wife glanced at the cattle-trader's widow, who was counting points in her hand. The judge's wife had noticed that the other woman had not been surprised that the Captain was late. Had she known?

'One heart,' said the cattle-trader's widow.

7

Over the next few days, the judge's wife found it difficult to think about anything other than the Captain's revelation that the boy had gone. It was to be expected that he would go – eventually – but she had not imagined that it would be easy for the Captain to get rid of him at this stage. She had asked the Captain about him at bridge, but she had not got much of a reply. Yes, he had gone, up to Lusaka. No, he had no idea what he was going to do up there. He had an uncle there, he thought, but he was not sure.

She raised the matter with the cattle-trader's widow, but she seemed unwilling to talk about it, and pointedly changed the subject. Then, at bridge one evening, the Captain suddenly produced a letter that he said had come from the boy. He fished it out of his pocket and read a few lines. The boy sent his regards to all of them.

The judge's wife noticed the stamp, and saw, she thought, that it had been posted in Lusaka. But she could not be sure.

'I'm relieved that he seems to be so happy,' she said. The Captain nodded, and put the letter back in his pocket.

The next day, she was driving past the Captain's house and called in on impulse. He offered her tea, which they drank on the veranda.

'The cricket team must miss him,' said the judge's wife. 'It is a bit odd that he should leave before their important match. I thought it was very strange, didn't you?'

The Captain lifted his teacup. 'At that age, you do that sort of thing,' he said. 'At least, I did.'

'But it seems so odd,' she said. 'Going off like that. Was everything all right between you and him? Sometimes I felt that, well, it was almost as if he was calling the shots.'

The Captain did not answer.

8

The judge telephoned the Captain the following day and asked him to come round to the house. He was distraught, and the Captain went straight away.

'My wife has gone,' said the judge. 'She's left me.'

'But ...' said the Captain.

'She left a letter,' said the judge, picking up an envelope and taking out a single sheet of paper. 'Look, here it is. She tells me that she's had enough of living here, and needs to start a new life. She asks me not to try to contact her.'

'Just like my wife,' said the Captain. 'I'm so sorry. It happened to me, too.'

The judge was staring at the Captain. 'It's very strange, though,' he said. 'This is a typed letter. My wife never typed. She couldn't.'

The Captain looked down at the floor, and then out of the window, past the trees on the judge's lawn, and the beds of Namaqualand daisies, to the mountains beyond. They were blue, impossibly blue, like islands in the sea.

Music Helps

1

La lived in a small town near the Suffolk coast. It was not Aldeburgh, but it was close enough, a town which had had a market, once, but which now had none of the bustle a market town has. It had an old church, built in Norman times, a thousand years or so ago, and several other beautiful buildings, including an old wool house which attracted visitors. There were farms nearby, some of which were rich ones, some of which barely scratched a living.

La came there in 1938, and started an orchestra. She was at that time in her mid-thirties, a tall, not unattractive woman, with a careful, measured way of talking. She had married young, barely into her twenties, and then had been widowed when she was thirty-two. Her husband had left her well provided for, but nothing could make up for her grief. I loved him so much, so much, she thought.

I can never love another man; no man will ever be his equal. None.

She bought a house outside the town, about half a mile down one of those quiet roads that wind through the Suffolk countryside. It was a large old house, with walls of wattle and daub, oak-beamed, and painted on the outside in that extraordinary soft pink colour that one sees in parts of the Suffolk countryside. It had large gardens, five acres or more, with lawns and a rather overgrown pond. Sheep had ruined part of the garden before she bought it, but she repaired the fence and kept them out. The sheep looked in, with grumpy expressions on their faces.

La started her orchestra after a friend suggested that they invite an orchestra from London to entertain them with a concert. La was feeling cross with London, because another friend had made a patronising remark about people who live in the countryside.

'No need to invite anybody from London here,' she sniffed. 'We're perfectly able to form our own orchestra.'

'Are we?' said one of her friends. She sounded doubtful.

'Of course we are!' snapped La, now quite convinced that this was what should be done.

'There's plenty of talent here. An abundance.'
She waved her hand airily in the direction of
the window.

Her friend looked outside. The lawns, over
which the evening sun was setting, were
touched with gold. There were two pigeons
cooing somewhere. But there did not seem to
be any orchestral talent.

Undaunted, La proceeded to speak to the
editor of the local paper. He listened to her
seriously. These people, he thought, come up
with some very odd suggestions, but this was
surely one of the oddest. Discreetly, unseen by
La, he scribbled on his pad: *La's Orchestra*.

2

At least the editor of the paper had the grace to
admit that he had been wrong. It turned out
that not only was there a great deal of musical
talent in the area, but it was talent of a
reasonably high level. A number of retired
players from great London orchestras offered
their services, and many others, some coming
from as far away as Cambridge, wanted to play.
It was, it seemed, a thin time in the orchestral

world, and the possibility of the occasional booking in return for dinner at La's house and a rail ticket to and from the concert was enough for many musicians. In the manner of a skilled manipulator, La knew how to persuade and encourage, and people found themselves committed to a far greater extent than they had bargained for at the outset.

Most of the players were not professionals, though they were competent amateurs. There were two, indeed, who had spent time studying music at academies, and some who could have done so, had life worked out rather differently for them. Then there was a handful of what were known as *the weaker brethren*. They, like those of a church congregation who were more likely to falter, were generously watched over by their more talented colleagues. Difficult passages of music were explained, tactfully, and, sometimes, whispered help was given: 'I'll do it. Just follow if you can.'

In general, though, this was not necessary, and the orchestra's performances were, by any standards, good and solid. On the orchestra's first anniversary, in May 1939, it gave a special concert. La basked in the glory – modestly, of course – inviting a great number of friends and giving a series of parties to mark the event.

Nobody minded her celebrating this triumph in the least.

But it was 1939. People asked: 'What about the orchestra, La? With things as they are . . . ?'

'We'll carry on,' she said. 'Isn't that what we're meant to do?'

So the orchestra continued during the war, and welcomed the talents of various musicians from the armed forces who were stationed in the area. An American airman livened up the percussion section for a brief and glorious period, and an accomplished Canadian violinist added real distinction to the string section for almost six months.

The orchestra performed concerts for the forces. 'It's not much of a contribution,' said La to a friend. 'But music makes a bit of a difference, I suppose.'

'But of course it does,' came the reply. 'It all helps.'

She pondered these words. *It all helps.* She had seen a man moved to tears of emotion at one of the concerts when they had played a piece by the composer Dvorak, and she knew that, yes, it was true. Music helped.

It was round about this time that La's Orchestra had its finest hour. A conference was being held in a country house. It was all very secret and the members of the orchestra, invited to play one evening to entertain those at this meeting, were taken to the venue without any idea of where it was. When they saw who was in the audience, they knew why.

The VIP was tired, and fell asleep briefly during one of the pieces. But afterwards, when he came to congratulate the conductor and the leader, he smiled and assured them that their presence had been important.

'Music helps,' he said. Then he produced a cigar from his pocket, waved to the players, and was gone.

3

La herself could not play an instrument. In the course of her somewhat chaotic education she had learned the basics of music, though, and her father had been good at the cello. He had encouraged her to take up the flute. But for a variety of reasons, this had never happened. The idea that she might one day play had remained unexplored. 'The flute,' she said, 'is the instrument I do not play.'

Her main contribution to the orchestra –

apart from acting as secretary, financial backer, venue organiser and tea-maker – was to copy out difficult-to-find parts, by hand. La somehow managed to borrow musical scores, but parts would often be missing and she would go to Cambridge, consult a library and copy the missing part by hand. She would spend hours doing this, her fingers becoming stained with black ink. But her copying of the notes was clear, and people liked to have La's parts to play from, with each page signed at the bottom: *La*.

She had the time to do this because she had no job. Of course, during the war years there was plenty for her to do. She drove an ambulance four days a week, releasing its usual driver for other duties, and she also did shifts at a small care centre where wounded servicemen were looked after. But for the rest, it was the orchestra that took up her time and energy.

Sometimes, in the early hours of the morning, La would wake up and worry about her orchestra. What would happen if the conductor could no longer conduct? He was getting on a bit, and he had complained about his heart. Conducting was sometimes vigorous work, and she imagined that it might put a strain on the heart. Perhaps this should govern their choice of music in future? Perhaps she should look at musical scores in advance and determine whether they were going to be a little bit too physically demanding?

What would happen if the unthinkable occurred? What if the country were to fall to the Nazis? What would happen to her orchestra? Would everyone be sent away, or just be forbidden to play? What if music were to be banned, to be declared some sort of threat? Her orchestra then might have to go underground, playing secretly in people's houses, racing through the repertoire in hiding with somebody standing guard outside, ready to give warning.

Such thoughts – ridiculous thoughts – made La turn on the light. Light dispelled such fantasies, such defeatism; light put them in their place. The country would not be overrun; Britain would hold out. It was impossible to imagine defeat, not because one could not imagine what it would be like, but because it was just such an unlikely outcome.

Everyone thought that, she told herself. She knew nobody who thought otherwise. Indeed, one member of the orchestra, a recently recruited Polish exile, had said to her, 'We will win this, you know. We will.' He had looked at her as if challenging her to disagree with what he had said. But she did not, of course, and the Pole had then said: 'You know why we will win? It is because music is on our side.'

4

This Polish exile, who was called Feliks, worked on a farm. He had been wounded, and limped as a result. This made him unfit for the army but fit enough to drive a tractor. He lived in a cottage at the edge of a large arable farm. The farm was owned by an elderly man who was something of a recluse. He saw Feliks once a day, gave him his orders and then disappeared back into the farmhouse.

Like La, Feliks was in his thirties, a quiet man who had lost confidence after his injury. He never spoke about what had happened to him, and La knew better than to pry. There were so many people around to whom terrible things had happened that it was better to wait until they chose to tell you, if they chose.

He had come to one of the concerts, and that was how she had met and recruited him. The concert had been in the hall of a school, and at the interval they had served tea from one of the school's large urns. La had been serving, along with two other women who helped her with these tasks. She had not noticed Feliks in the queue, but suddenly he was before her, holding out the tuppence that they charged for the tea and a small, rather tasteless biscuit.

She had poured his tea and passed it to him. He had taken the cup and it was then that she noticed his hand was shaking. The cup rattled in its saucer.

He saw her looking at his hand, and the shaking stopped. He moved away, but when La had finished serving tea she looked up and saw him standing by himself at the end of the room.

She folded up her apron and went up to him.

'I haven't seen you at our concerts before,' she said.

'No,' he said. 'This is the first time.'

He smiled at her as he spoke, and she smiled back. He was a foreigner, obviously, although his English was quite good. She asked him where he was from. He told her.

She thought: I would have said he was French, from the way he looks, but no, that would have been a mistake. The French were more self-confident than this man; he was shy and retiring in his manner.

'You obviously enjoy music,' she said.

He reached to put his cup down on a table at the side of the room. Somebody walked past him and bumped him slightly, and he blushed, as if he was embarrassed at being in the way.

'I do. Yes, I do.'

'We might play some Chopin again,' La said. 'We played a piece by him at the last concert.'

'That would be very nice.'

She noticed that he shifted his weight from foot to foot, as if in discomfort. Poor man.

Then he said, 'I play the flute, or I used to. I have not played for a year now. No, it's longer than that.'

This interested La. She said, 'You must tell me your name.'

5

La went to Cambridge by train one morning, leaving shortly after ten. It was summer but the day, which had started with sun and warmth, had become rainy. Great grey clouds had built up to the west, and she could see the rain in the distance, over the fields of Suffolk and Cambridgeshire, falling in shifting veils, like curtains. From the window of her train, through drops of rain on the glass, she watched an aeroplane flying in circles, lazily. A woman seated opposite her saw her watching and said: 'They'll be training. Just boys, you know. Mere boys. Eighteen, if that.' She shook her head in what could have been disapproval, or regret; La could not tell.

La said: 'Thank heavens for them.'

The train continued on its journey. Now Cambridge came into sight – familiar spires; well-worked allotments, every inch given over to growing food; a forest of bicycles at the train station. She had to walk to the shop, and it took her over forty minutes; the rain held off, but it was there, she felt, in the air, not far away.

'You telephoned me,' the man said. 'You're the person who telephoned?'

She nodded. 'That was me.'

He was standing behind the counter. He looked past her, through the window. 'Rain,' he said.

'Yes.'

'Well then,' he said. 'The flute.'

He turned round and opened a cabinet

behind him. He reached in and took out a narrow, leather-covered box, which he opened. 'Here it is,' he said. 'It's a very nice instrument. Would you like to try it?'

He handed her the flute. The metal was cold to the touch. For a moment, she saw herself, fragmented, in the silver. 'Try it? No, I don't play, I'm afraid. I'd like to, but I don't.'

'So it's for someone else? A child?'

She shook her head. 'It's for a man – a man who used to play but doesn't have a flute at present.'

'Then he'll be very happy with this instrument,' he said.

She left the shop, carrying the flute in an old shopping bag that the man had given her. It had not taken long to make the purchase – much less time than she had imagined – and this would give her the chance to do more of the things that she had on her list. But first, she wanted to shelter from the light shower which had started. There was a tearoom at the end of the street – that would do.

She took the last free table in the tearoom and ordered tea and a scone. Then she took the flute out of its box and examined it, holding it delicately. He would be surprised, of course, but it would make such a difference to him.

She knew the cottage he lived in because she used to drive that way often. It was rather a dark place, she thought, and the farmhouse itself looked a terrible mess, even from the outside. Not a cheerful place to be, even in summer. Having a flute would make it easier for him, much easier.

6

La decided not to warn Feliks that she was bringing him the flute. The evening after she returned from Cambridge, she rode her bicycle out to his cottage. The rain had played itself out, or moved on, and the air was filled with warmth. In the field next to his cottage, cows were standing close to the gate, chewing, gazing vacantly at the road. Flies buzzed at their eyes. They watched as she walked up the narrow path that led to his front door. He could be working, she thought, as there were still hours of light left, in which case she could leave the flute on his doorstep, with a note perhaps. Even if she were not to leave a note, he would know that the flute was destined for him, although he might not guess who had left it there as a gift.

But Feliks was in, and he answered the door almost immediately after her knock. He seemed surprised to see her, and for a moment he stood there, blinking, as if trying to remember who she was.

'This is for you,' she said, handing him the leather case.

He took it from her, gingerly. He stared at it, turning the case over in his hands. He looked up at her, somewhat puzzled.

'Open it,' she said. 'Go on. Just open it.'

When he saw the flute, he gasped. 'This is for me?'

She gave him an encouraging smile. 'You told me that you played. You said that you didn't have a flute. Well, now you do.'

He lifted the flute from its case and examined it carefully. 'It is very fine. Very fine.' He paused. 'But I cannot pay. Not yet. Maybe later.'

'Nonsense. This is a present. Consider it … consider it to be a thank-you present for all the work that you're doing here. Otherwise this place would be lying fallow.'

He nodded, showing that he understood. Then he lifted the flute to his lips, and without blowing, his fingers moved to a succession of positions. He was quick, light in his touch.

She looked past him through the door, into

the room behind. It was sparsely furnished – a table, a single chair, a wireless that Feliks must have got from somewhere. The farmer was mean – or so everybody said – and he did not provide any comfort for this man who worked for him. She frowned.

'May I play it?' He tapped the flute. 'It is so beautiful.'

'Of course. It's yours now. Yours to play.'

She listened as he played a tune she did not recognise. His playing was deft; he knew his instrument. She would invite him to join the orchestra; he was clearly good enough. When he had finished playing, she asked him whether he would care to join.

'Now that you have given me this,' he said, 'how could I refuse?'

'You could not,' she said. 'Or rather, you could, but it would be very rude.'

'In that case,' he said, smiling, 'in that case, yes.'

7

The following week, Feliks came for his first orchestral practice. La introduced him to the conductor and to the other flautist, and then went to the back of the hall where she sat during practice. 'Just ignore me,' she said, and they usually did. But she watched and listened, and knew the strengths and weaknesses of each player. The bassoonist had a weak sense of timing and occasionally came in too late, or too early, or sometimes not at all. The cellos were good; they never made any mistakes. The brass section had a tendency to be noisy and from time to time had to be asked to keep quiet while the conductor was explaining something. One or two of the violinists were hesitant in their playing, and the conductor would lean towards them in an exaggerated way, a hand cupped to his ear.

During the break, when the players were milling about at the end of the hall, she saw that Feliks was standing by himself, awkwardly alone. She had been talking to one of the brass players, but excused herself and walked over to her protégé. But just before she reached him, one of the violinists, a young woman whom she knew very little about – one of the transient, floating population of wartime – went up to him. La stood quite still. She saw this young woman smiling, sharing a joke with him, and the sight filled her with anxiety.

She pretended to be consulting her notebook, but she was watching. The young woman reached forward and laid a hand on his forearm in a gesture of reassurance, it seemed, or in the way in which one will emphasise a point. He was smiling, she noticed, responding to the young woman; smiling and nodding his head.

La turned away. She felt confused. Why should she be jealous of his conversation with this young woman? He was nothing to her; and yet she had gone to Cambridge to buy him a flute, an expensive present by any standards, and she had found herself strangely excited by the thought of giving the instrument to him. It was as if the gift bound them together in some way, which it should not because she did not want to be bound to anybody, not now.

At the end of the practice, La busied herself with administrative tasks: consulting the conductor about his diary, noting down dates, handing out a musical score. Then suddenly she was aware that Feliks was there, standing close to her, the flute case tucked under his arm. His clothing, she noticed, was poor. He had changed out of his working clothes for the practice, but the collar of his shirt was ill fitting and had been turned inside out to hide its age, she thought.

He looked at her, his gaze fixed on her, serious, almost reproachful.

'You are cross with me for some reason,' he said. 'You pretend not to notice me.'

She looked at him with what was meant to be astonishment. 'Of course I'm not cross with you.'

He went on. 'It's because I was talking to that woman, isn't it?'

La wanted to turn away. By what right does he imagine that I'm interested in him? she asked herself. Then he said: 'I was talking about the music we were playing. That's all.'

She stared at him.

8

He came to her house. It was in the evening, a few days after the practice at which they had had that unsettling conversation. She was in her sitting room, at the back of the house. There were still the last rays of the sun on the trees and the light had that faded, soft quality that one sees, almost feels, on a summer evening. Drowsy – she felt drowsy. The wireless was on, bringing the news from those far-off places, now so familiar, that some people marked on little maps pinned to their walls.

She suddenly became aware that there was somebody in the garden, coming round the side of the house. She heard him first, his footfall on the gravel, a crunching sound, and she stopped dozing. Nobody came that way, at least not in the evening. Sometimes the butcher's boy would come round and leave his parcel at the kitchen door if there was no reply to the bell, but otherwise nobody.

In her slightly confused state, she thought: this is something to do with what's happening; this is something to do with the war. But then she realised that was ridiculous. She rose to her feet as she heard the footsteps again, closer now. When she saw him through the French windows, it took a moment for her to recognise who he was, he was so unexpected. Her first thought was: how does he know that this is where I live? She had not told him.

Feliks's eyes met hers through the glass, and then he smiled and made a gesture. He was wearing a cap, a grey cap, which he took off. There was something in his other hand.

She moved towards the door and opened it

to him. The evening air flooded past her, warm on the skin.

'I hope I didn't frighten you.' His voice was quiet.

'No. Not really. Surprised me, though. The front door ...' She trailed off. She saw that what he was carrying was the flute in its leather case.

'I knocked at the front door. But then I heard the wireless inside and I knew that you must be in.'

She gestured for him to enter the room, and he did so, wiping his boots on the mat carefully, taking his time. He looked at her with an expression that she did not know how to interpret, though it seemed to her like apology. He handed the flute to her.

'I've brought this back,' he said. 'I can't accept it. I can't take it from you, and I cannot pay for it. I ask you to understand.'

The flute was in her hands now, and she stared down at it, uncertain what to do. Of course he had his pride; that was it – she had heard people say that the Poles were proud. She could understand. When your country was taken over, invaded by another, you must hold on to your pride, or the small scraps of it which remain.

She thought quickly. She wanted him to have the flute. She wanted him to play in the orchestra. Suddenly that seemed so important.

An idea occurred. He could work in her garden for her. He could earn the flute; it would be a fair exchange.

9

She became used to seeing him. He came three days a week, in the evenings, and set about his work in the garden. He knew what he was doing, she discovered; he knew the botanical names of the plants, which was far more than she did, and he seemed to have an understanding of their needs. He harvested lavender – her namesake – for her, and tied it in bundles, upside down, to dry. At the end of the path, where there had been weeds, it was now neat and well tended. He planted new things, moved others to better spots. 'You must be careful what you plant in the shade,' he said.

Afterwards, when he had finished, she watched him walk down the road with that halting gait of his, and felt lonely. But I can never allow myself to fall in love with him, she said to herself. I'm finished with that.

The orchestra was going through a period of particular energy and enthusiasm. They were working on a programme for a concert they were going to give in December which was ambitious and some of the members found difficult. La attended every rehearsal, and watched Feliks playing his flute. He smiled at her, almost in conspiracy.

'You get on well with your Polish flautist,' said one of the cellists. 'A good discovery, from every point of view.'

La said nothing, but smiled. Orchestras always liked to gossip; *people* always liked to gossip.

The conductor said to her, privately, at the end of a session: 'It was a good idea, La, getting that man along. He has a lovely playing style, doesn't he? The flutes are a joy now.'

She felt proud of her discovery. When December came, after the concert, which proved so popular that two performances were arranged, she invited Feliks back to the house for a meal. He accepted, and they sat in the dining room, Feliks somewhat uncomfortable in a suit that she had not seen before, a grey affair with wide lapels.

'When this is all over,' she said, 'what are you going to do, Feliks? When you have Poland back?'

'*If* we have Poland back,' he said. 'There are many people who might not want that.'

She was silent. 'But it's going our way. It really is. Look at Sicily. Look at Italy.'

He looked thoughtful. 'We can play Italian music again,' he said, 'and not feel uncomfortable about it.'

She laughed. 'I never felt uncomfortable. Mussolini and his gang don't belong there. This is not what Italy is about.'

He smiled. 'You are British,' he said. 'You believe that everybody is good. I'm Polish. We look at things differently.'

She inclined her head. She was not sure whether he had paid her a compliment, or otherwise. But he had not answered her question, and so she posed it again.

He shrugged. 'I shall see how things are. I'm comfortable here, in this country. I like not being frightened of people in uniform. I like warm beer that tastes like ...' he made a face. 'I like your little orchestra.'

La listened.

10

They knew before it happened. It was clear enough, although there were setbacks, when the Allies met with resistance and things slowed down. But it was obvious now how things were going to end, and people felt a quiet satisfaction – just that. There was no triumphalism – people were too tired, too worn down. But soon it would come to an end, and the nightmare would be over.

Feliks had long since paid for the flute with his work in the garden, but he insisted on coming still, especially now that it was spring, or almost, and the garden needed a lot of work. La watched him from her sitting room, and took him mugs of tea.

'I've been thinking of something,' she said to him one day. 'Do you think it's bad luck to plan for something in advance? Before it happens?'

He seemed to read her thoughts. 'Like victory?'

'Yes. In particular, a victory concert. It might happen at any time, you see, and the orchestra must be ready.'

He brushed some soil off his fingers and wiped his hands on his trousers. 'A very good idea. We should plan it. But I have one request. Can we play something Polish? Please. I know it's your victory, but for us, too, we have struggled ...'

She readily accepted his suggestion. They started to practise, although nobody said what it was for. They all knew, though, that this concert would be a special one. When the day came, suddenly, dramatically, they made posters and put them up within hours. The orchestra was ready.

The programme was a long one, because La knew that nobody would want it to end. The hall was packed; people stood at the back, their arms on each other's shoulders. They embraced, and at the end instruments were laid down and the members of the orchestra shook hands with each other. They smiled at each other.

Feliks walked with La back to her house. She stopped outside the door. He smiled at her and held out his hand. 'You have been so kind to me,' he said.

They shook hands.

'What will happen to the orchestra?' he said. 'Now that this ... this is all over?'

They had not spoken about this before. She knew, though, that it would be difficult. People would leave, would move on. The orchestra would probably not continue. The conductor was too old now and would not want to carry on, now that the country was at peace, or almost at peace.

'I'm afraid that it will probably fold up,' she said. 'It's had its day. Sad, but there we are.'

'It could carry on,' he said. 'Life will go on.'

She smiled at him. 'Yes, life will go on. But I have to be realistic about the orchestra. We've had a good time. We really have.'

He sighed. 'Oh, well.' Then he turned and walked down the road. He did not see her expression.

11

It had been so difficult to travel, but now she could. She decided that she would go down to Cornwall, where her cousin lived. They had not seen one another for some years, and in that time her cousin had married. She wanted to meet the man whom she had only seen in photographs.

She spent three weeks in Cornwall, staying in the house that her cousin and the new husband lived in at the edge of a village. Her cousin grew vegetables and kept hens; La ate large mushroom omelettes for breakfast, making up for the years when it had been difficult to buy eggs. In the mornings, when she woke up, her cousin's husband brought a tea tray and put it beside her bed.

'You're spoiling me,' she said.

'You deserve it,' he replied. 'You've been working so hard.'

Have I? she asked herself. Hardly. Not hard compared with others, with people on convoys, in the mines, in factories. The cousin's husband himself was a doctor. He worked in a hospital nearby, and had done so through the war.

'And your orchestra, La?' said her cousin. 'Tell us about your orchestra.'

'It does its best,' she said. 'Some of the players are very good. Others are, well, enthusiastic.' She paused. 'I think that we probably won't continue. People are leaving. Giving up. I suppose they've had enough.'

The cousin looked sympathetic. 'Understandable.'

On the way back, on the train, she found herself thinking of him, of Feliks, and looking forward to seeing him again. She had brought some cheese for him from Cornwall because she knew that he had a weakness for cheese.

She let herself into the house. There was a pile of mail on the floor, and she saw his handwriting on one of the envelopes. She knew immediately what it would say; that it was his goodbye note. She opened it quickly, tearing the top of the cheap notepaper inside. 'I have had to go immediately,' he wrote. 'There are not many jobs for us now, but I have been given one up in Glasgow. There is a Pole there who has a senior position in a fertiliser firm. He has offered me a job. It's too good a chance to miss, and I have to take it up immediately. So I have left without saying goodbye, in person, without thanking you for everything – for your friendship to a stranger, for the flute, for your orchestra. Yes, thank you for your orchestra. Maybe people don't say thank you for orchestras, but I do. Thank you.'

She put the note down on a table and walked through to her sitting room. The air was stale, the air of a house that had been closed up. She went to the French windows and opened them. She remembered the evening that she had opened the doors to him, and how the air had flowed into the room at that moment, so warm.

12

La was right about the orchestra. The conductor called off the next rehearsal – he wanted a break, and she understood. Perhaps they would start again in the autumn, or even the winter, he said, but she knew that this would not happen.

She missed Feliks to begin with; she missed the war, in an odd sort of way. It had given her purpose, something to do. Now there was no ambulance to drive and no call for volunteers. Nor was there much work for her. She began to help out at a riding stable nearby, although she did not really like horses very much. It gave her something to do, and she became involved in the affairs of the stable.

The years passed. She went to concerts, in Cambridge and sometimes in London. But she did not like the grime of the city, the second-hand feel of the air, and so the trips to London became fewer and fewer. She looked in the mirror. She was now in her fifties, although she looked younger. I could still get married, she thought, but there were no men, and she was not prepared to look for one. I am destined to live my life here, in this quiet corner, not doing anything in particular. If we each have a moment in our lives, a time when we count for something, mine was when I had my orchestra. La's Orchestra. How many people can claim to have an orchestra named after them? That was an achievement – that was something.

Then, in 1959, she decided to treat herself to a trip to the Edinburgh Festival. It was the most glittering of the festivals, and she had seen the programme. She splashed out on the best tickets for the big concerts; she booked a room at the North British Hotel, a room with its own bath.

She went to the opening concert in the Usher Hall. She was sitting in the fifth row from the front, among people who were formally dressed: dinner jackets, long dresses. They were elegant people from New York, London, Geneva. She felt out of place; she had stayed in rural Suffolk too long. During the interval she went outside to get some fresh air, and that was when she saw Feliks. He was standing under a light on the steps, reading the programme notes.

She wanted to embrace him, but did not. They looked at one another, discreetly, assessing the impact of the years. He looked the same: smarter, of course, but otherwise unchanged.

There was so much to say. He told her that he was in the same job, but more senior. He was a manager now, and had a share in the business. He had done well.

'Any family?' she asked hesitantly.

'I am divorced,' he said. 'Some Catholic, but there you are. She left me. I have a son. He is six. He stays with me.'

'You must come and see me,' she said. 'Come down sometime. Bring your little boy.'

He gave her his address and a telephone number.

'How about you?' he said. 'Same place? Same house?'

'Yes,' she said. 'The same.'

13

She had hoped that he would contact her, that he would at least telephone, but he did not. She almost telephoned him on several occasions, but stopped herself. If he had wanted to be in touch, then he would have been. She should not pester him.

In 1960 she went to Italy for a month. She travelled as far down as Naples, where she was robbed. Everything was stolen: her passport, her money, her camera. She did not feel bitter; in fact, she was surprised at how calm she felt. That is because nothing happens in my life, she said to herself. This is the most dramatic thing that has happened in years, and so I don't really mind it. A friend said, 'You're very philosophical, La. If that happened to me, I'd be furious. Incandescent.' La smiled; the word made her think of Vesuvius, the volcano at Naples.

Then, the following year, something happened. It happened a long way away, across thousands of miles of ocean, but it seemed to La as if it were happening right next door, as if, oddly, it were personal. An American spy plane, cruising high over the Caribbean, photographed a missile installation in Cuba. Suddenly this was in the news; grave words were uttered. She read a front-page article in a newspaper which said: *This is very, very serious. This could be the end.*

La read this and thought of what the words *the end* meant. They meant the end of the trees on her lawn, of her old house, of the lanes that ran into the countryside, of the hedges at their sides, of the innocent air, of the high, empty skies of her part of England. It meant the end of the village pub, of the butcher's boy with his bicycle, the end of London, of the radio, of music.

On that first night of the crisis La could not sleep. She lay there in the darkness and looked at the ceiling. It would come quickly, they said. There would only be, what? a four-minute warning. Four minutes. What could we do about it? She reflected on the fact that you couldn't do anything once the build-up started; you couldn't come face to face with the people concerned and say *stop*; or go down on your bended knees and implore them not to continue. You could not, because the people concerned were hidden behind doors and walls; they were deep in bunkers, behind concrete, far away. You could not speak to them.

She got up at four in the morning, not having slept at all. She had decided, and the decision survived the turning on of her light. She would hold a peace concert, urgently, in a few days' time. She would gather her orchestra. She would pay their train fares. She would bring the orchestra together – for one last time – in a concert for peace. It didn't matter if nobody heard it or took any notice. It would have happened. They would have done something.

14

She wasted no time in telephoning the members of the orchestra. Some of them could not be traced, of course; some were dead, or had not been heard of for years. But word got out, and one would telephone another. Slowly the sections came together and agreed: yes, they could come and play in the concert. 'It will be pretty much a scratch performance,' said La, 'maybe one rehearsal.' Nobody minded that. They would be there.

She telephoned Feliks last because she at least knew exactly how to contact him, and because she had been anxious about it. He was silent for a few moments after she had explained to him what it was about.

'You want me to come, don't you?' he said.

'Yes,' she said. 'I'm asking you to come.' She felt that it was almost as if she was calling in a favour, but she wanted him there, she particularly wanted him there. 'Bring your little boy with you,' she said.

'I will,' he said.

They arrived. She watched old friends catching up and exchanging addresses. She thought, if it doesn't work, if there's no peace this time, then those addresses will simply cease to exist. It's different this time.

They managed one rehearsal, a brief one, and then the concert took place. Word had got round, and people came; too many, in fact, with the result that they had to open the doors of the hall and let people listen from outside. La sat at the back of the hall, as she always did, and at her side was Feliks's little boy, now eight. He behaved well, holding a small toy car that he played with discreetly on his knee, driving it up and down. She glanced down at him and smiled. He smiled back.

She had forgotten the various performances of her orchestra and so she couldn't judge whether it was better now than it had been before, but it sounded beautiful to her, so beautiful, very much what she had wanted it to be. At the end of the concert, when the last notes had died away, there was utter silence in the hall. Then, one by one, the orchestra stood up, and so did the audience. They stood up in complete silence. Nobody said a word, nobody coughed or shuffled feet; there was just silence. Then they went out. It seemed that everybody felt it was wrong to break the atmosphere of the moment by applauding, and so there was no clapping. Just silence.

La went outside and looked up at the sky, where there was still a glimmer of light. Feliks's little boy was with her, but she had almost forgotten him. He does not understand, she thought, which was just as well.

15

She had put Feliks and his son in the spare room at the end of the corridor downstairs. When she awoke the next morning and went into the kitchen, she saw that the two of them were already up and out in the garden. Feliks was showing his son the shrubbery, which reminded her that he had planted some of those shrubs, still there after all those years.

He wanted to show his son where he had lived, and so he took him off after breakfast, in his car. She stayed behind. She was giving coffee to a number of members of the orchestra who had travelled down for the concert and would be leaving later that morning.

'Well,' one of them said, 'I hope that helps. I doubt it, though. Isn't it awful?'

'Music helps,' she said. 'Even if ... even if ...'

But she could not bring herself to finish the sentence.

Then they heard the news. It came on the radio, in the kitchen, and it was shouted out. Somebody said, quite simply, *peace*. She sat down because she thought that she would pass out. She held her head in her hands. 'Oh,' she said. Just: 'Oh.'

She wanted to find Feliks immediately and tell him, but she made herself wait until he came back. Then she went out to the driveway. He saw her through the window of his car, and she realised that she must smile or he would think that it was bad news. She smiled. Then, to underline the point, she waved her hands in the air.

He said, 'Good news? Is it good news?'

'Yes,' she said. 'Yes.'

He turned round and embraced his young son and kissed him. The boy looked surprised, even embarrassed. Then Feliks took La's hands in his. He did not kiss her, but squeezed her hands, as if sharing some secret good news.

'Your orchestra, La,' he said. 'Your orchestra saved the world. Again.'

She thought about this later. He had said *again*, and then she knew what he meant.

They went inside, where she had made

coffee. The last time they had been together there had been no real coffee; now, such luxury. There would still be coffee, and water to make it with, and people to drink it. Those things had been threatened, but now the threat was gone.

'When do you have to leave for Glasgow?' she asked.

He hesitated, and she realised that there were times when something must be said, something wildly inappropriate – forward, really.

'Don't go,' she said. 'Stay. Just stay. We could get the orchestra going again.'

He looked at his son, and then looked back at her. She rose to her feet and picked up the little boy and kissed him.

Quick Reads

Books in the Quick Reads series:

Amy ...
Beverley Barber ...
Bloodmoney ...
Buster Fleabags ...
The ...
Chickenfeed ...
Cleanskin ...
The Choice ...
Cleo Peace ...
A Cool ...
The ...
Doctor ...
Doctor ... Africa ...
Don ...
Doctor ... Fever ...
Doctor ... Rescue ...
Lady ... the Rose ...
A Dream ... Time ...
Follow ...
Hell ...
Girl ... Yesterday ...
Girl ... Rome ...
The ... man ...

Quick Reads

Books in the Quick Reads series

Amy's Diary	Maureen Lee
Beyond the Bounty	Tony Parsons
Bloody Valentine	James Patterson
Buster Fleabags	Rolf Harris
The Cave	Kate Mosse
Chickenfeed	Minette Walters
Cleanskin	Val McDermid
The Cleverness of Ladies	Alexander McCall Smith
Clouded Vision	Linwood Barclay
A Cool Head	Ian Rankin
The Dare	John Boyne
Doctor Who: Code of the Krillitanes	Justin Richards
Doctor Who: I Am a Dalek	Gareth Roberts
Doctor Who: Made of Steel	Terrance Dicks
Doctor Who: Magic of the Angels	Jacqueline Rayner
Doctor Who: Revenge of the Judoon	Terrance Dicks
Doctor Who: The Sontaran Games	Jacqueline Rayner
A Dream Come True	Maureen Lee
Follow Me	Sheila O'Flanagan
Full House	Maeve Binchy
Get the Life You Really Want	James Caan
Girl on the Platform	Josephine Cox
The Grey Man	Andy McNab
Hell Island	Matthew Reilly

Hello Mum	Bernardine Evaristo
How to Change Your Life in 7 Steps	John Bird
Humble Pie	Gordon Ramsay
Jack and Jill	Lucy Cavendish
Kung Fu Trip	Benjamin Zephaniah
Last Night Another Soldier	Andy McNab
Life's New Hurdles	Colin Jackson
Life's Too Short	Val McDermid, Editor
Lily	Adèle Geras
The Little One	Lynda La Plante
Men at Work	Mike Gayle
Money Magic	Alvin Hall
My Dad's a Policeman	Cathy Glass
One Good Turn	Chris Ryan
The Perfect Holiday	Cathy Kelly
The Perfect Murder	Peter James
Quantum of Tweed: The Man with the Nissan Micra	Conn Iggulden
RaW Voices: True Stories of Hardship	Vanessa Feltz
Reading My Arse!	Ricky Tomlinson
Star Sullivan	Maeve Binchy
Strangers on the 16:02	Priya Basil
The Sun Book of Short Stories	
Survive the Worst and Aim for the Best	Kerry Katona
The 10 Keys to Success	John Bird
Tackling Life	Charlie Oatway
Traitors of the Tower	Alison Weir
Trouble on the Heath	Terry Jones
Twenty Tales of the War Zone	John Simpson
We Won the Lottery	Danny Buckland

Lose yourself
in a good
book with *Galaxy*®

Curled up on the sofa,

Sunday morning in pyjamas,

just before bed,

in the bath or

on the way to work?

Wherever, whenever,
you can escape
with a good book!

So go on...
indulge yourself with
a good read and the
smooth taste of
Galaxy® chocolate.

Quick Reads

Fall in love with reading

Quick Reads are brilliantly written short new books by bestselling authors and celebrities. Whether you're an avid reader who wants a quick fix or haven't picked up a book since school, sit back, relax and let Quick Reads inspire you.

We would like to thank all our funders:

We would also like to thank all our partners in
the Quick Reads project for their help and support:

NIACE • unionlearn • National Book Tokens
The Reading Agency • National Literacy Trust
Welsh Books Council • Welsh Government
The Big Plus Scotland • DELNI • NALA

We want to get the country reading

Quick Reads, World Book Day and World Book Night are initiatives designed to encourage everyone in the UK and Ireland – whatever your age – to read more and discover the joy of books.

Quick Reads launches on **14 February 2012**
Find out how you can get involved at www.**quickreads**.org.uk

World Book Day is on **1 March 2012**
Find out how you can get involved at www.**worldbookday**.com

World Book Night is on **23 April 2012**
Find out how you can get involved at www.**worldbooknight**.org

Other resources

Enjoy this book? Find out about all the others from
www.quickreads.org.uk

Free courses are available for anyone who wants to develop
their skills. You can attend the courses in your local area.
If you'd like to find out more, phone 0800 66 0800.

For more information on developing your skills in Scotland
visit www.**thebigplus**.com

Join the Reading Agency's Six Book Challenge at
www.**sixbookchallenge**.org.uk

THE
READING
AGENCY

Publishers Barrington Stoke and New Island
also provide books for new readers.
www.**barringtonstoke**.co.uk • www.**newisland**.ie

The BBC runs an adult basic skills campaign.
See www.**bbc**.co.uk/**skillswise**

THE NO.1 LADIES' DETECTIVE AGENCY

Alexander McCall Smith

The multi-million bestselling phenomenon

If you've got a problem and no one else can help you, then pay a visit to Precious Ramotswe, Botswana's finest – and only – female detective and proud proprietor of the No.1 Ladies' Detective Agency. Her methods may not be conventional but she's got warmth, wit and intuition on her side, not to mention Mr J. L. B. Matekoni, the charming owner of Tlokweng Road Speedy Motors. She's going to need them all as she sets out on a trail that will lead her into some sticky situations and more than a little danger in this first novel in Alexander McCall Smith's much-loved series.

Abacus
978-0-349-11675-4

Discover the world of Alexander McCall Smith
and sample his other books at

Alexander McCall Smith.co.uk